THOUGHTS FROM AN AGE
FROM ADOLESCENCE TO ADULTHOOD

THOUGHTS FROM AN AGE
FROM ADOLESCENCE TO ADULTHOOD

BY
MICHAEL STRAHLMAN

To those closest to me - my loved ones.

To my friends, my family;

to my darling wife

&

our two beautiful children.

CONTENTS

Michael Strahlman

ABOUT THE BOOK

Well, here it is. Part I of my anthology of creativity; a collection of poetry and songs.

I had always dreamt of writing a book of poetry, from when I first started writing in my teens. I loved experimenting with basic wordplay and concepts to paint a picture; and I always found the medium of poetry to be a poignant way to express something complex in my life in a simple way. So, one poem down and immediately ambitious (aged 15), I thought, "Why don't I write book of amateur poems and call it 'Poetry 101 - 101 Poems'? How ironic!".

...obviously that didn't happen. Firstly - a hundred and one poems is a TON. Secondly - the 'irony' turned out to be rather trite. I had thought that somehow, the irony would make it less serious - yet more thought-provoking - but I continued to surprise myself at the breadth and depth of my thoughts. So...I parked it.

At the same time, I started writing songs for guitar, piano and voice, branching out from the classical music I was playing day-in / day-out.

The songs, initially filled with teenage angst, brought out a new side of me; an expression of myself that at the time wasn't visible to most. In writing music, again ambitious, I dreamt of writing albums; performing; sharing my thoughts with the world. In the end - I chickened-out - favouring a more 'traditional' career path vs. the creative side.

...and so, I continued into adulthood, reaching time-to-time to my guitar or notebook, often in the middle of the night, to annotate my life and let out creative steam in the midst of the grind. For a long time - the absence of my creativity as a dominant feature in my daily life gnawed at me. Something about creating, and impacting with the world, wasn't being achieved. In particular, I was struggling to share it with those who inspired me most.

Over the past few years, this sensation has germinated, and the idea evolved into that of building a creative "legacy". I realised, full of ego, that what really was missing for me was to answer the question: once I'm gone - what of this, my thoughts, creativity, will be left behind?

I realised that rather than "impact", it was important to me for the words to be permanently left behind.

...and so: that is how this book came to pass.

I now dream that one day - when paper books are 'obsolete' - one of my grandchildren will find this little paperback on a shelf of 'relics', blow some dust off it, and say, "Grandpa - what IS this?". I'll laugh, sit them down, and read aloud a selection of psalms plucked from the inner recesses of my mind.

In a way, this collection has unconsciously become a catalogue of my thoughts / hopes / desires / dreams from between the ages of 15 through 30(ish). The true inner anxieties, feelings, memories and concepts I have felt and shaped into the words are on the pages to follow. With that, I invite you to take a look and see how things evolved.

My thoughts from an age...

Michael Strahlman

PART I - POETRY

(1)

BLINK

(2002)

The blue/grey swirl of a wistless age
spins round indefinitely –
round the Milky Way.
Passengers on the train of life
sit idly
as their journey lurches to a stop:
destination reached (the end of the line).
Among those lost, some found
comfort in the rumbling
of train-to-track –
(click-clack) –
The sound numbing, mesmerizing,
Clouding the clatter of common conformity
and closed their eyes.
The blue/grey swirl of a wistless age –
blink, and miss it.

(2)

TICK-TOCK

(2002)

Tick-tock
the clock methodically paces the day
whilst wishes press its gears
to burst and delay.
The clock won't slow,
nor stop, nor pause
for a break whilst
you do.
Schedules and tables – revolving
around it, struggle fruitlessly
to add a 13
or a 25, even.
The mind ticks too
as time bombs do –
but this count is down
not up
'till the time runs out.
But the clock keeps
ticking, tocking;
never stopping.

(3)

THE HUNTER

(2002)

Silent, sleek, smooth:
the hunter stalks its prey.
Inch by inch it creeps,
blending into its surroundings –
as a killer in disguise
it approaches.
Silence – a tension, lightning
rigid in the air coils
with sinew and muscle
to pounce and savage
its goal.
A crimson mist replaces
the stagnant, humid air
and the hunter bathes
in the warmth ensued.
Red-raw and ragged
the hunter takes his due
and retreats to the shadows –
on its own
once more,
the silent assassin.

(4)

THE MEADOW

(2003)

A bird flies high across the meadow;
the echoing beating of crow's wings
splits the silence
of the morning sky.
An awkward cry
from a new-born sends
shooting rockets from their nests,
while fawning mothers' chests
soothe and give life,
restoring peace from the din
of startled youths'
eyes closed again.
A breeze whips the tall grass
lazily on its side,
as a lover would confide
or profess, even.
The wind's whisper warns
of storm and young ones' slumber
interrupted,
but comforted as to a mother's touch;
to dream again.

(5)

THE RAIN

(2003)

A sea of green blanketed
the horizon
as a lazy rain fell.
Two days since the
red spray of battle –
the land was cleansed of sin
once again,
as the heavens washed away
the stains and scars of war –
a holy gift granted to nature,
as a penance for human
injustice.
As drip-dried dregs drained
away, an uncanny beauty
sparkled in the setting sun –
a new tinge of redness in
the sun-setting sky –
a resolved peace.

(6)

GRANDPA

(2003)

The man sat in his rocking chair,
whistling an age-old tuneless melody,
beckoning me.
His skin wrinkled with a smile
and tough as old leather,
but a warmth of love all the same
as his hand took mine.
His green eyes playfully twinkle
ever knowing – a look of ageless
wisdom and caring justifies the silence.
His figure muscular and tender
as he lifts me into his arms –
I gaze in wonder at his growing
smile, and sink deep into his
loving grasp.
I remember the days when I
crawled into his arms and sat
for eternity, and sometimes I
wish for them back.

(7)

PASSENGERS

(2004)

Light glinted off her golden hair
as the sun set.
A shimmer of color dazzled in the dusk
as a wash of rainbow striped me.
Her eyes as oceans knocked me to
the ground and she fell in a heap
beside me.
The sand was the promise of ecstasy;
my desire reflected in her eyes.
I clasped her hand and a tingling spread
through my spine like a brush fire – igniting
emotion coiled up inside me.
As my lips touched hers I felt her heart
flutter
and she pulled me close.
Hand in hand we walked along
the rippling tide
and faded –
just passengers in the
night.

(8)

AUTUMN

(2004)

Crisp, cold discarded leaves
littered the ground on this autumn morn –
the air briskly whipped,
and our turned-up
collars hugged our faces.
The sky was a bright tinge of orange
through the golden canopy – leaves
changing colors glowed with the sunlight
of a new day.
A blush of warmth felt on your cheeks –
a sign of weather, or the perk of
the longing beating of your heart.
Eyes closed, the smell of frozen dew
and broken hearts' leaves
crash through the senses
flittingly.
I see us hand in hand, in a park,
or on a bench – carefree as time
rolls by.
Crisp cold leaves discarded
like pages of a memory, yet to be
a whim or woe or want is uncertain.

(9)

HER (1)

(2005)

The stars shone brightly in the night sky
as darkness fell.
All was silent – but not without tension,
anticipation of the excitement yet to come.
Suddenly, the doors burst open, and a
flood of energy and warmth enveloped the
night.
A sea of smiling faces, laughter – a satisfaction
and happiness has been created here.
Why is this?
Beyond the doors
lies a stage set with blazing neon lights,
whilst the players, now exhausted in the wings
let out sighs of relief and pride as they
rest.
One more than all however, above the rest
shone brightest that evening.
Her manner; demeanour; courage;
brought tears to my eyes.
A special actress, a special evening –
the beauty of her words and self
magnificently thrust upon the world
open armed – to share this gift
is to make a difference.
You have made that difference;
you have won my heart.

(10)

NOTRE DAME

(2005)

The echo reverberated,
crisp and clean as a
wash of holy cadence cleansed me.
Dimly lit, the walls of the
place rose above as I
held my breath – tensely
poised for the next entry.
Slowly and silently the sound
grew and crescendoed into
heavenly proclamation; to silence
once more.
The blissful sound of praise
penetrated the awe-inspired
magnitude of the place,
to leave a lasting impression and
gratitude – a connection, the sliver
of Him for that moment will last
forever within my soul.
I cast my memory back:
remembering,
being –
the humblest reverence of our
lives.

(11)

HER (2)

(2005)

The sky twinkled around me
as I knowingly entered – hands empty
in the place of love.
The aura carried upwards with the
lifts as the surrounding lovers
silently caressed.
Her perhaps knowing (or even not)
that I was with her, and my
soul an open book for her to leaf –
my rum-candied breath releasing
me from boyish inhibitions and solemnities.
A wayward traveler clung fiercely
to her cheek as we moved to the abyss –
in my eyes I calmed it soundly, with
the familiarity of a long-practiced dance.
Even with my love in the shadows that night,
I felt at peace,
one with the sparkling Parisian skyline;
empty handed still, yet
fuller in the heart.

(12)

SPENCER

(2005)

5' 9", sandy hair, and a
sly twinkle in his green eyes
describes him best – carelessly yet
strategically sprawled on the lounger.
Some might call it provocative;
I know better.
We chat for hours on seemingly nothing
yet in that same seamless manner
bridge the gap of time with an unforced
ease.
I feel he is like me (hopefully)
in the sense that he radiates
warmth and kindness, while
his wit and humour are unrivalled.
His gift is that of song,
and he can jazz his way through anything.
A shoulder to lean on,
(perhaps a Kleenex too)
he is always there for me.
Call me old-fashioned, but he is,
quite simply,
my best friend.

(13)

THANK YOU

(2005)

> Thank you for your
> heart in its sadness, and your
> anger in its madness.
>> (Thank you for your)
> naiveté, and your
> kindness all the same.
> Your overwhelming
> opacity at times is sovereign, but
>> (most of all)
> your unrelenting ability to make it
> Better serves you best.
> every day I ask for
> callous forgiveness of my
> kindred sins to you.
> you never need ask back.
> Would you have known?
> Over bef-
> ore its chance.

(14)
HER (3)

(2005)

Are you afraid?
Or is it the reflection
of my feelings off your
mahogany exterior.
Like a shell to crack
or even a slippery
lobster claw you escape
my tender grasp.
Impenetrable, fortress-like
you deflect my obvious
feeling like to anesthesia.
My pride broken;
my time spent (wisely?
I don't think so).
Are you scared that
someone like me could
get close?
Or are you afraid of
being alone?

(15)

THE FERRY

(2005)

The spray of salty mist
scattered my dreary senses.
I stared at the retreating shoreline,
rhythmically dancing
stilly
against the rocking rails.
As the chalk-white cliffs faded,
a low fog settled as
an uneasy mask of weather.
Bitter, cold wind lashed
the salt and brine
against my unshaven face,
as I braved the elements
to have my space.
I felt my senses numb
and I closed my eyes –
swaying in time with this
lonely rollercoaster
I found a sudden clarity,
clearing the haze in my mind.

(16)

FAILURE

(2005)

Failure – a demon,
writhing serpent inside us all,
incessantly pressing at
cracks in our seams.
Try as we may to subdue
the beast, he mocks our plights,
and inevitably
punctures and breaks the surface.
Our biggest weapon is our
hearts; but also, our biggest weakness –
it will triumph always,
over time,
but in our darkest hour (it seems)
it never will.
It is our hope, our own guiding light,
but will it carry me
out of the deepest crevices of my mind?

(17)

TENDER ROSE

(2009)

Tender rose -
a chance was theirs to dream,
remembering the
lips
pain tore apart.
Being fate to fancy such
men from Eden -
the heart's sweet abyss
pushed fickle flights and
fled from your mind.
I hope she remembers me one day
upon red tempting sheets
where the cruelty of night
melts to day - a
quarrelling of senses,
bodies rising,
passion meeting at a knife tip.
The pull of the song
torments me,
and yet as the dawn breaks
we must rise and start again.

(18)

SISTER (1)

(2009)

I am so proud of you.
Your strength, courage,
uncertainty,
spirit -
there are great things to come.
Have faith -
this gravity cannot be resisted for long
and once harnessed
you shall
be filled with possibility.

Believe in yourself,
as I believe in you.
Believe
in your creativity,
your vision, your power to affect and
make change.
Believe in your soul and hope and joy
because however dark the world seems
this light will always guide you.

I am always here to
hear you,
to hold you,
to keep you safe;
to help carve your path
(if you'll let me)
and support you.

Sister - warm kindness with
sight beyond her years.

(19)

BRIGHT AND SHINING BLUE

(2014)

Bright and shining blue -
enchanting -
colour dancing in the moonlight.

Your eyes capture my imagination,
make me smile,
take me with you on our journey
when I once was lost in life.

My companion, my lover, my friend -
the days are long and fresh
with each waking moment I am with you;
each moment asleep I yearn for you.

Together you have shown me
felicity
I never knew was possible. A love
so deep
so wide
so...magical - my heart aches
so full to the brim of you.

Forever, my love, will I be with you
and
forever, my love, will I be true to you.
Now more than ever,
muru.

Of time, my present, my future:
my bright and shining blue.

(20)

I AM A LOVED ONE

(2015)

(I am:) a loved one
(I am:) your youngest son
(I am:) a musician, an artist
(I am:) humbled.

(I am:) who you taught me to be
(I am:) in awe of your being
(I am:) a cog in your great machine
(I am:) a part of your legacy.

You are my father
You are my trusted friend
You are my loyal companion
You are my wise old sage.

(You were:) a Renaissance man
(You were:) so fierce and strong
(You were:) so sharp, so proud
(You were:) so simply - brilliant.

(You were:) our leader
(You were:) our teacher
(You were:) a part of our team
(You were:) the spark that lights the room.

You were: so frustrated and scared
You were: so frail, so small
You were: so brave
(and then) you were: gone.

I am so
grateful
for those moments so big
and so small.

I am so
blessed
to be part of this family -
which you made.

I am a loved one -
because:
you
taught me.

(21)

PAS ENCORE

(2015)

Hold my hand.
Hold it
tightly.

Take it - I said,
don't forget to hold
tightly.

Take my hand,
I cried,
I'm losing you - there's slack.

Don't let go yet,
my love,
there's still time (you'll see).

Don't leave me
here,
I'm not ready yet.

I don't know how
to be
alone, (my dear).

Stay with me now,
mon père,
n'est pas possible; pas encore.

These tears, these tears.

These tears well up, and
release
that last sigh: goodbye.

I don't know
what to do
without you.

(22)

SISTER (2)

(2011)

Fortune fades away
but time,
time grows stronger.
With your heart still beating -
what is your fear - what holds you back
so you cannot see yourself clearly any longer?

Grow strong.
Search
the vast 'scape for direction
and inspiration.
Hollow promises will hold
for a time
but this fortune waits for no one.

Promise yourself you'll build strength
from within,
and tackle your
daemons
with righteousness.

Good luck girl;
be strong;
hold tight
to your dreams.

(23)

LA SANGRE

(2010)

Strangers -
at once dissimilar,
unfamiliar,
yet not a stranger on the path of life.

A meeting of the minds
(albeit brief)
side-by-side at the flask-edge,
pushing and building each other's dreams.

The time spent righting the world;
the stark realisation that with both
truths and faults:
life is a game;
a game played (most often) without conscious.

Recognise: things happen for a reason,
and this life,
my life,
is pulling you to the path you believe in.

Life is not unfair
and will test you -
but the choice is always yours.

Amigo, igual en todo y
con el temperamente de mi
hermano de sangre.
Todo la vida; "la sangre".

(24)
HAPPINESS

(2011)

What is it?
In the ether -
something not quite there,
yet
is floating,
drifting,
just outside your reach; and is
so beautiful.

What is it?

Happiness
is like chasing butterflies
...perhaps no one wants to admit
when they have it;
or have found it -
once you catch it, you let it go
(or jar-it on a shelf in your bedroom).

Is happiness like chasing butterflies:
a game left behind as you grow up?
Is it only for children?

Adults distract themselves,
possibly endlessly,
to avoid it
or
the truth -
not that they would be unhappy,
but the truth is what happiness truly means -
and therefore the result
and reality
of hard choices.

(25)

FATHERHOOD

(2016)

How will I be?
Will I be strong,
tough,
or kind?

Will I know how to love you
when the time comes?
Will I know how to teach
when you are lost?

Will I know how to hold you -
so tight -
so gently -
when you are brand new?
Will my love be unrequited
or fierce
and pure?

What awesome power -
a gift, yet curse -
to know I will shape this life
even before it is born.

Sometimes I fear;
I cannot know
how
to be a father
before I know the whole of
myself.

Can I know how to
be
before I
am?

What I do know
is
I am ready to try.

(26)

MORTALITY

(2016)

What makes a man regret?
If not regret - what makes a man
feel?
When did the clock turn faster,
seasons blurring,
colliding,
merging,
into one relentless epoch;
suddenly opening your eyes
to see
the end of the line?

Astonishing
to hear
anger
at age.
To feel
rage
(at a concept)
of nothingness.
When did all this time pass -
now with curtains poised to fall.

Beware the quickening pace,
the shortening of time and space -
each new day
a smaller portion;
a smaller sample
of the rich and full tapestry of life,
nearing the knot of completion.

I thought I knew what they looked like.
I thought I knew each shape and line on their faces.
I thought they would stay the same,
forever
etched in my mind
in stasis.

When did it happen?
When did their hands thicken and fingers bend?
When did the cracks and creases
begin to appear?

I am scared
to hear
of the mortality of life.
To hear this from my one so strong.

I never thought I'd (yet) meet it face to face.
Perhaps, with this first brush,
I have met my time-worn friend.

(27)

LOST TIME

(2016)

Tears,
hot and wet,
for the time lost;
for the time we are unable to get back.

How an instant - a moment -
can change all moments
without prejudice,
irrevocably.

Lost are the moments
of youth,
of knowing someone so completely
through sacred propinquity.

Tears,
fast and sleek,
for the time spent;
for the time played out as string.

They fall in those times of weakness;
reflection;
resentment;
feelings never meant to stay underneath.

Was it not a happy time?
Blissfully unaware of the pain of others?
A time wondered differently
with the wisdom of age.

Tears,
long and deep,
for the time gone;
for the time now lost at sea.

The time,
I suppose,
was not just lost
for me.

(28)

SPACEMAN

(2016)

Spaceman -
floating in space,
pushing off the walls
to make contact with us beyond.

Bumps and kicks
and tweaks and licks;
and twists and flips
and bends and jerks.

Dancing baby within the womb,
learning to grow,
to breathe,
to hear the sounds of the world outside.

For now, in cocoon,
suspended;
one day you'll join us
out here in the world.

Until then,
little spaceman,
keep on kicking
and
we'll meet you soon.

(29)

FRAGMENTS

(2016)

Fragments, snapshots,
fortuities, memories -
a dance (or game)
to find your place.

Create the space
to be;
play in your band -
your own symphony.

Too much stimulus;
too much greed;
too easy to fill
time without need.

Make choices wisely -
true friends indeed -
together you'll stand,
together - you'll see.

Hit your stride now,
n'er bend the knee,
with sangfroid you'll walk
paths yet unseen.

To the edge,
to the end,
and to all
in between.

(30)

BLOSSOM

(2016)

Blossom:
frost broken;
ground broken;
hearts broken
and burst open
with the promise of new life.
The earth is renewed
and growing with the change of seasons.

I see you growing too;
hear the rapid beating
of your tiny heart.

I see her growing,
changing,
becoming something we dreamt of -
hoped for;
dared for
in hushed whispers in the night.

This bud will blossom and change;
it changes us more than we yet know.

But:
that first breath -
every breath new -
a miracle.

PART II - SONGS

(1)

YOU AND ME

(2007)

You and me - we are what we used to be
(I say) you and me - what are we?

Why are we taking chances carelessly?
Really I should be just not free.

You are wanderin' so carefree
in and out of my mind.
I take you hand so trustingly -
you're gonna take control of me.

Innocent - we were that once (oh) back when
but now I see - you've come for me.

You are wanderin' so carefree
in and out of my mind.
I take you hand so trustingly -
you're gonna take control of me.

Complacent - sittin' on my heels just waiting
for you to come and take me places I've never been.

You are wanderin' so carefree
in and out of my mind.
I take you hand so trustingly -
you're gonna take control of me.

(2)

SOMETHIN' NEW

(2007)

The rainfall was light, it never felt better.
It felt right - the simple pleasure.

I was compelled, a sense of adventure.
That one night we were together.

I want you to hold me beside you.
You take me higher and higher - a new view.
I want you to know somethin':
I think you can show me somethin' new.

I can't decide - a hopeless endeavour.
Your maverick aside - I don't know what's better
('cause:)

I want you to hold me beside you.
You take me higher and higher - a new view.
I want you to know somethin':
I think you can show me somethin' new.

Why can't it be?
What have you done to me?
I cannot see -
what it means...

I want you to hold me beside you.
You take me higher and higher - a new view.
I want you to know somethin':
I think you can show me somethin' new.

(3)

SHADES OF GREY

(2002)

My eyes have seen a time,
with the past not far behind -
footsteps on the fine line
between wrong and right.

Can I finally find my sign
standin' out through space and time?
With the strangers in the future:
the thick and thin of life.

Just my shades of grey, shades of grey - honey.
In my way, come what may.
Oh my time of day - the price I pay
for those shades of grey.

On a cracked and crooked spine,
running down that back of mine.
Shadows all around me
fade to distant light.

As I try to learn what's mine
and figure out if that's my crime -
all my words my crimson vanity
not just black and white.

Just my shades of grey, shades of grey - honey.
In my way, come what may.
Oh my time of day - the price I pay
for those shades of grey.

(4)

LOST WITHOUT YOU

(2008)

Once every day
you helped me find my way.
I can't complain,
just wished you'd stay.

I learned so much,
your wisdom in my soul.
It's not enough -
you make me whole.

I'm scared now and you are gone.
Beyond repair now and I'm alone.

The day we met,
I was innocent.
Without regret (of)
each day we spent.

I'm scared now and you are gone.
Beyond repair now and I'm alone.

I know it's true:
I'm lost without you.
I know it's true:
I'm lost without you.

What's left to do?
I'm lost without you.
Can't face the truth -
I can't breathe without you.

I'm scared now and you are gone.
Beyond repair now and I'm alone.

(5)

SUBLIME (WHAT'S MINE)

(2005)

I loved you once,
you hurt me twice -
when the night falls, on my own
I'll cry.

I lost you once,
but now you hide -
in that nightfall, on your own
time flies.

You cannot take my pride.
You cannot break my smile.
I'll find love again in time.
I want you to know what's mine.

Will I ever find
what's left in this life?
Only nightfall, on my own
will I fly.

You cannot take my pride.
You cannot break my smile.
I'll find love again in time.
I want you to know what's mine.

I don't know why
Your reason for crime.
I've paid the price -
will I find sublime?

Will I survive?
Can't I revive
that nightfall? Once more
I'll try.

You cannot take my pride.
You cannot break my smile.
I'll find love again in time.
I want you to know what's mine.

(6)

ONE WEEK

(2005)

I woke up Monday early morn
scattered dreams of Sunday torn.
Broken promises - they foster this
fleeting premise in the afternoon.

You whispered softly in my ear.
Whispered I should never fear.
Wednesday here at last, Tuesday is the past
as we lie here in the middle of the room.

You turned my world upside down
but I'll land two feet on the ground.
'Cause one week's enough to trip and fall,
and I don't know you at all.
I don't know you at all.

Pull me close, hold me tight.
Just one more kiss tonight.
Simple fantasy, shrouded in mystery;
my suitcase packed I can't be here with you.

You turned my world upside down
but I'll land two feet on the ground.
'Cause one week's enough to trip and fall,
and I don't know you at all.
I don't know you at all.

Night and day - you take me away.
(But them) seasons change - and my heart still
beats the same.

One week is gone.
Now I'm back where I belong...
...'cause one week's enough to trip and fall
and I don't know you at all.

You turned my world upside down
but I'll land two feet on the ground.
'Cause one week's enough to trip and fall,
and I don't know you at all.
I don't know you at all.

(7)

WHY CAN'T I FEEL THIS WAY?

(2004)

Why do I see you in my heart?
Deep inside me in my soul -
a part of me I can't escape.
If I had the chance to make things right,
to end my silence - cease my fight.
We'd never be apart.

Tell me why can't I feel this way about you?
Why can't I feel this way?
As out paths divide behind me,
and the storm begins to grow.
Tell me why can't I feel this way about you?
Why can't I feel this way?
(Oh) you said you loved me –
then you walked right out the door -
don't go.

Time - a deepened shadow - black on white,
has no mind to know what's right,
though it feels like yesterday.
(Oh time) a wedge between us and to spark
that angry fire in the dark
I should have known it from the start...

Tell me why can't I feel this way about you?
Why can't I feel this way?
As out paths divide behind me,
and the storm begins to grow.
Tell me why can't I feel this way about you?

Why can't I feel this way?
(Oh) you said you loved me –
then you walked right out the door -
don't go.

I know it's true - it's me loving you.
What can I do?
But you can't remain - I can't let you stay.
What can I say?

Why can't I keep you from my mind?
Felt in everything that's mine;
etched in stone inside my heart.
If I could take back what tears have cried
and redefine my senseless life -
I'd say I love you here tonight.

Tell me why can't I feel this way about you?
Why can't I feel this way?
As out paths divide behind me,
and the storm begins to grow.
Tell me why can't I feel this way about you?
Why can't I feel this way?
(Oh) you said you loved me –
then you walked right out the door -
don't go.

(8)

ONCE UPON A DREAM

(2004)

I watched you walk across the room
your smile shined out of the gloom.
You came from where - oh I'd never dare.
On golden wings - I tried not to stare.

Could it be? Just another dream.
Was it me? Better than it seems.
Could I be...

...could I be dreaming
...oh dreaming
...could I be dreaming about you now?
...could I be dreaming
...oh dreaming
...was it once upon a dream? (Better than it seems)

I watched you dance that endless dance;
you caught my gaze; go you touched my hand.
I saw you there; I kissed you there;
I smiled as the sunlight sparkled off your hair.

Could it be? Just another dream.
Was it me? Better than it seems.
Could I be...

...could I be dreaming
...oh dreaming
...could I be dreaming about you now?
...could I be dreaming
...oh dreaming
...was it once upon a dream? (Better than it seems)

Oh I wish it were so
How it goes so easily!
As I toss to-and-fro
and think restlessly...

...could I be dreaming
...oh dreaming
...could I be dreaming about you now?
...could I be dreaming
...oh dreaming
...was it once upon a dream? (Better than it seems)

(9)

I WANNA KNOW

(2005)

I wish you were here beside me.
Did you go disappear - was it me?
I wish you could hear
(deny me back, deny me back)
I see things so clear
(I'm off the walls, without a cause)

(But you) my dear my heart.
You my dear my heart.

I wanna know what love is.
I wanna know why you care.
I wanna know - I wanna know!
I wanna know what's there.

Why can't things steer clear
(of chaos and disorder)
(and) although you carry fear –
I need you back, I want you back
(and) through the haze and steel –
could it be?
Clarity so near –
it's haunting me, disturbing me

(But you) my dear my heart.
You my dear my heart.

I wanna know what love is.
I wanna know why you care.
I wanna know - I wanna know!
I wanna know what's there.

You are beyond compare.
I'm feelin' G-d-damned scared.
The love and anger - the flash of anger -
how can it be repaired?

I wanna know what love is.
I wanna know why you care.
I wanna know - I wanna know!
I wanna know what's there.

(10)

BLIND

(2003)

I have your heart
tucked away in me.
Alone, untouched - but wanted:
the fire of ecstasy.

When you wake up alone in your bed
your eyes have yet to see.
When your heart turns from love to regret
your soul to misery.

Oceans apart
a distance we cannot meet.
No time to spare for loved ones
all ends in blood and tears.

When you wake up alone in your bed
your eyes have yet to see.
When your heart turns from love to regret
your soul to misery.

I'm so blind
I cannot see.
How I've tried
but we cannot be.
I'm so blind.

Two lives about to start
breaking up piece by piece.
They drift, avoid - all's ended:
confirming all my worst fears

When you wake up alone in your bed
your eyes have yet to see.
When your heart turns from love to regret
your soul to misery.

I'm so blind
I cannot see.
How I've tried
but we cannot be.
I'm so blind.

(11)

IN MY ARMS AGAIN

(2001)

I see you, I feel you
in my arms again.
I want you, to hold you
in my arms again.

I know there'll be sun
but the rain shall fall.
I know I'll meet someone -
I'm not sure at all.

My hear mine, your eyes drive
the fire of my mind.
Fly soul, fly - go unwind
in my arms again.

I know there'll be sun
but the rain shall fall.
I know I'll meet someone -
I'm not sure at all.

I miss you, ache for you
in my arms again.
Deep wounds you, inflict you
in my arms again.

I know there'll be sun
but the rain shall fall.
I know I'll meet someone -
I'm not sure at all.

I miss you, ache for you
in my arms again.
Deep wounds you, inflict you
in my arms again.

(12)

THE LOVE I LOST TO YOU

(1999)

I'm rememberin' the past down that twistin' path
and the look on her face makes it all come back.
I want you to know how I feel.
I want you to know how I feel.

For the love that I lost
makes the world come down.
Down that road of glory,
lies and deceit.
For the love that I lost
brings my life into view.
For the love I lost to you.

When you soul's fire's alight
you'll guide me tonight.
I take a look through your eyes
and I wish for your sight.
Can you give me just one more chance?
Can you give me just one more chance?

For the love that I lost
blocks my mind from your view.
When the depths of your darkness
shine out through your eyes.
For the love that I lost
breaks my heart in two.
For the love I lost to you.

I'm rememberin' the past down that twistin' path
and the look on her face makes it all come back.
I want you to know how I feel.
I want you to know how I feel.

For the love that I lost
blocks my mind from your view.
When the depths of your darkness
shine out through your eyes.
For the love that I lost
breaks my heart in two.
For the love I lost to you.

(13)

CHANGE

(2001)

It seems my life is gonna change.
Change just like the leaves do turn,
why could it not stay like this for me?
You are the only one for me.
Perfect in every way I see,
why could no-one else be right for me?

My love is pure, my heart is sure:
the only one for me.
To end my strife, you changed my life:
the only one for me

It's always been so very strange.
Strange as love shows twists and turns –
to overcome them seems too hard for me.
And then I see your smilin' face.
Wind blows through your gentle hair,
your eyes and mine lock - this is love for me.

My love is pure, my heart is sure:
the only one for me.
To end my strife, you changed my life:
the only one for me

It seems you've changed my life for me.
Change as our time slows and burns
to ash on ash we say our prayers for thee.
And when all ends you're my mem'ries.
Together there we'll ever be,
our hearts entwined our love beats pain - you'll see.

My love is pure, my heart is sure:
the only one for me.
To end my strife, you changed my life:
the only one for me

It seems my life is gonna change.
It seems my life is gonna change.

(14)
FRACTURED

(2006)

Can you walk down that line
knowing you cannot return?
Can you take that one chance
and brave your heart's commands?

I am fractured, broken and scared.
Can you capture that moment to spare?
Time will pass us and no-one cares.
I'm alone here - I'm alone

One true life, one true time -
can you ever know what's right?
Just one test of your faith
and to see if you're alive.

I am fractured, broken and scared.
Can you capture that moment to spare?
Time will pass us and no-one cares.
I'm alone here - I'm alone

Am I strong enough, will I be enough
to see my one desire?
If I'm not strong enough, will I be enough
to live with the lie?

Find the light, can you try
to remember you can fly?
Will you break your defense
and create your final plan?

I am fractured, broken and scared.
Can you capture that moment to spare?
Time will pass us and no-one cares.
I'm alone here - I'm alone

(15)

YOU STILL HAVE ME

(2007)

When all is lost,
your life incomplete.
When darkness falls
and your eyes cannot see.

When you need strength,
when you need faith:

You still have me.
You still have me.
When you don't believe -
you still have me.

The road is long,
no end can be seen.
To carry on
or admit defeat?

When you need strength,
when you can't breathe:

You still have me.
You still have me.
When you don't believe -
you still have me.

Take my hand - trust in me.
Make your stand - let it be.

In the end time,
it will heal.
Feel gently soul -
not this time, you won't break.

When you need strength:
I am here.

You still have me.
You still have me.
When you don't believe -
you still have me.

(16)

JAILBREAK

(2000)

My possessions are all I dreamed of,
my life and path (in) disarray.
I find myself lonely, unheard of -
but ambition is here to stay.

I've got the sunshine.
I've got the moonlight.
You are my heart's crime -
my jailbreak to my life.

I left my last hope for another,
a girl I first met on the street.
Love at first sight thought absurd of -
she felt not, nor knew what to say.

I've got the sunshine.
I've got the moonlight.
You are my heart's crime -
my jailbreak to my life.

I have strength yes I pray,
I have hope not dismay,
for that chance for an escape -
(oh) I feel it every day.

I've got the sunshine.
I've got the moonlight.
You are my heart's crime -
my jailbreak to my life.

Eyesight and hindsight forgive me,
my heart set in stone in one day.
Though I've got a hole in my pocket -
I won't let you get away.

I've got the sunshine.
I've got the moonlight.
You are my heart's crime -
my jailbreak to my life.

(17)

WHERE ARE WE NOW

(2000)

Myself and I alone
in a place that I call home,
I've turned my self inside-out -
where are we now?

I run empty - slow,
lyin' down face-first in snow,
with the ice that burns inside-out -
where are we now?

Where are we now, where are we?
I'm deep inside now I cannot see.
I'm lost and blind now, you're stuck in me -
where are we now?

While the fates still play their games,
I never leave this empty stage.
When the lies have turned inside-out -
where are we now?

Life around me now has changed
to a wrong and crooked stave,
where the music cries to die now -
where are we now?

Where are we now, where are we?
I'm deep inside now I cannot see.
I'm lost and blind now, you're stuck in me -
where are we now?

(18)

FOR HER I SING

(1998)

Morning light shines from within
my day, my life shall soon begin,
with laughter, love, she is to bring,
from her, for her I sing.

My heart, my mind, my soul combined:
she is my ideal friend.
She's blessed my life her love will find -
from her, for her I sing

Myself I see myself in her,
to her I feel the same,
my life, my dreams, and all in between -
I see herself in me.

My heart, my mind, my soul combined:
she is my ideal friend.
She's blessed my life her love will find -
from her, for her I sing.

(19)

FIX ME

(2009)

Where did I stand?
When did I fall?
When did you mean nothing at all?

Can't I pretend not to feel small?
Can't I be real
and answer the call?

I'm falling apart,
I'm falling to pieces.
Am I still dreaming of nothing at all?
I'm falling apart,
I'm falling to pieces.
Can't you please fix me?
Fix me - my broken heart.

Try as I fight it
my daydream has ended.
Closing in and crushing me.

I'm so damn tired -
I'm lost at sea.
It's me.

I'm falling apart,
I'm falling to pieces.
Am I still dreaming of nothing at all?
I'm falling apart,
I'm falling to pieces.
Can't you please fix me?
Fix me - my broken heart.

That heart of mine - it's you this time.
Can you see me?
Can you feel me?
Can you hear me calling out your name?

All at one
must I have all the answers
to be what I'll be...yeah.

I'm falling apart,
I'm falling to pieces.
Am I still dreaming of nothing at all?
I'm falling apart,
I'm falling to pieces.
Can't you please fix me?
Fix me - my broken heart.

(20)

A REASON

(2011)

Why do you feed me those lies?
If I knew them, I'd be more wise.
Why did you leave me tonight?
Now I need you with me - holding you so tight.

Do you have a reason, a reason to be here?
Do you even hear me asking please?
I'm tired of waiting to find your answer.
Do you even want to stay with me?

Turn your back away from me.
My heart aches when you
spin your circles thoughtlessly.
Lock the door and lose your key.
Whenever you leave me,
you take away what's left of me.

Do you have a reason, a reason to be here?
Do you even hear me asking please?
I'm tired of waiting to find your answer.
Do you even want to stay with me?

(21)

FREE

(2003)

Once I fell asleep in your arms
our hearts they beat anew as one.

But then you took away my pride.
With that you stole, afraid, my heart.

What do you hold over me my love?
Why can't I be free my love?

I woke in despair, hurt - impaired.
A fire in the air - nobody cares.

What do you hold over me my love?
Why can't I be free my love?

Why can't I see in your eyes?
Why can't I be in your heart?

You left in the night cloaked and scared.
I thought you just might be just right - the one.

What do you hold over me my love?
Why can't I be free my love?

(22)

BE FREE (ONE DAY)

(2008-2015)

I never thought I'd believe
the words out your mouth.
I never thought that the rain
would ever come down.
(With you) the truth is an answer
that'll never be found.
If you trust me one day you'll see...

One day we'll be blind enough to see.
One day we'll be blind enough for you and me
to maybe find enough for peace.
And then you'll find in us the will to be free.

Burnt to crisp at creation –
ignition complete.
Now our path is unstable –
we'll never come clean.
Should we turn on our heels now
and make our retreat?
If you trust me one day you'll see...

One day we'll be blind enough to see.
One day we'll be blind enough for you and me
to maybe find enough for peace.
And then you'll find in us the will to be free.

Too much shit for salvation –
could the blind man redeem?
Fight the fight of tomorrow
and break our defeat.
Curb our pride and our progress –
to make ends meet.
If you trust me one day you'll see...

One day we'll be blind enough to see.
One day we'll be blind enough for you and me
to maybe find enough for peace.
And then you'll find in us the will to be free.

(23)

CHASING BUTTERFLIES

(2012)

I waited all night,
baby it's not right,
and I need you by my side.
Baby it's alright,
I've got you tonight,
and I need you by my side.

I'm waiting for something,
but you've been right there from the start.
I'm waiting for something to lose -
it's you.

I want to kiss you, I don't want to miss you,
without you it falls apart.
I want to be with you, while I wait here just for you,
I need you inside my heart.
I'm chasing butterflies,
I'm chasing butterflies
I'm chasing butterflies - to be with you.

When you first met me,
I wanted you next to me,
to be in your arms so tight.
But I was empty,
waiting so patiently
to begin a whole new life.

I waited for something,
but you've were right there from the start.
I waited for something to lose -
it was you.

I want to kiss you, I don't want to miss you,
without you it falls apart.
I want to be with you, while I wait here just for you,
I need you inside my heart.
I'm chasing butterflies,
I'm chasing butterflies
I'm chasing butterflies - to be with you

That day you found me,
you opened your heart for me,
you told me everything's alright.
You held my hand softly,
the touch that completed me,
and I knew everything was right.

I waited one last time - for you.
And I waited one last time - one last time.

I want to kiss you, I don't want to miss you,
without you it falls apart.
I want to be with you, while I wait here just for you,
I need you inside my heart.
I'm chasing butterflies,
I'm chasing butterflies
I'm chasing butterflies - to be with you

Baby it's alright,
I've got you tonight.
Now you're here right by my side.

(24)

BEFORE OUR TIME

(2011)

You know I want you there.
I can't breathe without you there.
You know I can't compare.
I need you everywhere.

I know, let's go,
I know - it's true.

Time is on the wrong side.
Now it's gone - before our time.

What I see in the mirror,
my heart beats that much clearer.
One last touch; one last kiss.
Goodbye hurts now you mean it.

I know, I have to go,
I know - it's true.

Time is on the wrong side.
Now it's gone - before our time.

Try to fight tears I shed,
no room for things unsaid.
Beginnings and one's end -
behind us: time well spent.

I know, I must go,
I know it's true - because:

Time is on the wrong side.
Now it's gone - before our time.

(25)

HOME

(2013/2014)

Lost. It's where I am without you.
I don't want to be without you. Tell me
how to close that space between us,
the way I can complete us –
and you'll be (home)

Come on home,
I don't want to be, want to be alone.
You're the only one,
so won't you come on home?

Gone. You're so far away,
so damn far away from me.
But in my dreams, you are there by my side,
holding hands beneath the blue sky –
and we'll be (home)

Come on home,
and I'll never be, won't have to be alone.
You're the only one,
so won't you come on home?

Take a chance again:
take me home.
Now it's time to start again -
take me home.

Home. It's where I lay my head down,
I don't want to lay my head down - lonely.
Home - home is where my heart is,
and wherever that my heart is –
you'll be (home)

Come on home,
I don't want to be, want to be alone.
You're the only one,
so won't you come on home?

Come on home,
and I'll never be, won't have to be alone.
You're the only one,
so won't you come on home?

(26)

LAST DANCE

(2011-2015)

When I go, I know this much is true.
When I see you,
my heart it can't stop beating.
Breathe together now, lift your head somehow,
be the driving force that you're feeling.

(Here we go)
Hold tight don't let me go,
'cause I'm here and now
try to let it show.
This is our last chance,
This may be our last dance tonight.

Carry on - step by step each day.
Look through your eyes,
the world it won't stop turning.
Sing together now, find your feet somehow,
just in time to start believing.

(Here we go)
Hold tight don't let me go,
'cause I'm here and now
try to let it show.
This is our last chance,
This may be our last dance tonight.

Just be strong and fight that fight once more.
Girl I need you –
you're all that stops me bleeding.
Hold her steady now; take control somehow.
In your mind it holds the key.

One more time now just for me.

(Here we go)
Hold tight don't let me go,
'cause I'm here and now
try to let it show.
This is our last chance,
This may be our last dance tonight.

(27)

REMEMBER ME

(2016)

Could I ever be the one,
be the one to be?
A pretender in the sun
just outside my reach.

The familiar place
you'll never find me.
In the empty space
you'll never see.

(Tell me) why did I wait so long?
(Tell me) how did I trip and fall?
Now that my time has gone,
will you ever remember me?

Could I be the perfect one,
or just another bee?
Will I change, or will I run -
to let myself be free?

Time to set the pace;
pave the way to find me.
No more second place;
new day, new me.

(Tell me) why did I wait so long?
(Tell me) how did I trip and fall?
Now that my time has gone,
will you ever remember me?

What is left when we're all done,
you've left for all to see?
Take my chance - make history.
Make my legacy.

Now we're face-to-face:
today you'll find me.
Life is not a race -
just wait and see.

(Tell me) why did I wait so long?
(Tell me) how did I trip and fall?
Now that my time has gone,
will you ever remember me?

(28)

EVOLUTION OF LOVE

(2007-2016)

A boy walks down the street
unnoticed smile and awkward feet (he walks)
up to the girl he'd like to meet
stretched out his hand, says, "come with me"
(we can)

Grow older,
love bolder,
(Oh) it's you - who knew?
The evolution of love.

Time has passed, a fast romance
our little boy, now on one knee (he asks)
for her hand - forever more
up he stands: a boy no-more
(he says)

Grow older,
love bolder,
(Oh) it's you - who knew?
The evolution of love.

Time - it bends,
it can break,
it makes us change.
(But) this love - ever new,
makes mistakes,
and knows it's place -

to be the same;
ever the same with you.

Now our man walks down the street
a wave, a smile - picks up his feet (he lifts)
up his child into the air
this selfless love - beyond compare
(they sing)

Grow older,
love bolder,
(Oh) it's you - who knew?
The evolution of love.

(29)

BORN

(2016)

When you told me,
my heart forgot its place.
That day you found me;
that day you made me.

When your hearts beat,
that spark - it grows with pace.
The way you're showing,
that way you carry me.

You were one;
I was one;
now we're not the only ones.
When you're born,
I'll be born.
You're the one we're waiting for -
when you're born.

When you first breathe,
that cry - that breath you take.
That day, your story;
that day you changed me.

You were one;
I was one;
now we're not the only ones.
When you're born,
I'll be born.
You're the one we're waiting for -
when you're born.

We're not alone.
We'll start again, you'll see.
We'll make our home.
A brand-new family.
(Oh) baby.

When you hold me
I'll start to fill the space
you gave me; the whole of me;
that day you'll say to me:

You were one;
I was one;
and now we're not alone.
When you're born,
I'll be born.
You're the one we're waiting for -
when you're born.

(30)

ROUND AND ROUND

(2003)

Round and round
Never fall, never let
go and I
never stop, never let
go and I
must never let go.
Go and I
must never let go.

and I...

Need it so I cry
Need it so I lie
Need it so I sit down and sigh,
sit down and die.

I'm so high
and my head's in the sky
never drop,
never fall, never stop.
Fall and I
must never let go.
Fall and I
must never let go.

and I...

Need it so I cry
Need it so I lie
Need it so I sit down and sigh,
sit down and die.

ACKNOWLEDGMENTS

You made it - look at you! Well done. Thank you for indulging me and sifting your way through the inner workings of my mind (over the course of almost 15 years). You honour me.

I'd like to thank my parents for their encouragement and unwavering support over the years. They have been the best listeners, and more often than not, a source of my inspiration. Thank you for always pushing me to follow my dreams.

Thank you (grudgingly) to the women who aren't in my life - who shall remain nameless. Clearly, you caused me enough grief to pour my heart out across my teenage years. At least SOMETHING came of it.

Thanks to my siblings - all six of them - for forcing me to find my place amongst the craziness. You've all taught me so much, and like it or not, have molded me into who I am today.

Thank you to my closest friends - suffering through my angst and coaching me through thick-and-thin. Banter aside - thanks for stomaching my 'creativity' in its various shapes and forms. My number one fans!

Most of all - thank you to my darling wife. Without you, this wouldn't have happened - period. Thank you for pushing me to turn my dreams into reality, and for showing me the different ways to make that possible. You are my rock and my everything.

To little "Sesame" and "Pickle" - good luck trying to figure this all out when you're old enough.

INDEX

Printed in Great Britain
by Amazon